Take another ten

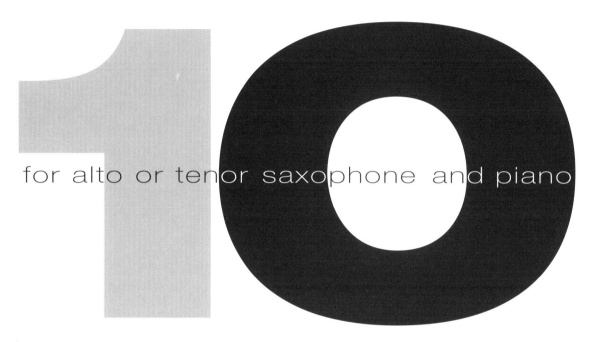

for alto or tenor saxophone and piano

arranged by James Rae

www.**universal**edition.com

vienna · london · new york

UE 21 170

ISMN 979-0-008-06752-5
UPC 8-03452-01610-6
ISBN 978-3-7024-1894-6

Preface

Following on from the success of the original Take Ten series, Take Another Ten is a further collection of popular concert pieces for the intermediate player. Once again I have chosen a wide range of compositional styles ranging from Bach to the present day which I feel will demonstrate the great versatility of the instrument. The accompaniments have been designed to be both approachable and musically supportive. I have also included chord symbols to enable the pianist to elaborate on the written accompaniment.

Parts are included for both Alto and Tenor saxophones.

Vorwort

Auf den Erfolg der ersten Reihe Take Ten folgt nun eine weitere Sammlung von beliebten Konzertstücken für fortgeschrittene Spieler: Take Another Ten. Wiederum habe ich mich für eine breite Palette von Kompositionsstilen von Bach bis zum heutigen Tag entschieden, da ich glaube, dass dadurch die große Vielseitigkeit des Instruments am besten zum Ausdruck kommt. Die Begleitungen wurden so geschrieben, dass sie sowohl leicht zu spielen sind als auch musikalische Unterstützung liefern. Ich habe zudem Akkordsymbole hinzugefügt, um dem Pianisten die Möglichkeit zu geben, seine eigenen Ausarbeitungen anzufertigen.

Zur Partitur gehören Stimmen sowohl für Alt- als auch für Tenorsaxophon.

Préface

Après le succès remporté par la première série Take Ten, le recueil Take Another Ten, rassemble de nouveaux morceaux de concert célèbres destinés aux instrumentistes de niveau moyen. J'ai sélectionné ici encore un large éventail de styles s'étendant de Bach à la musique actuelle qui souligne la grande diversité d'expression de l'instrument. Les accompagnements ont été conçus d'accès facile tout en fournissant un solide soutien musical. J'ai également inséré des chiffrages d'accord pour donner au pianiste la possibilité d'enrichir l'accompagnement écrit.

Des parties de saxophone alto et de saxophone ténor sont incluses.

James Rae

Contents

It Don't Mean a Thing
(if it ain't got that swing)

Duke Ellington
(1899–1974)
Arr. James Rae

Air on a G String

Johann Sebastian Bach
(1685–1750)
Arr. James Rae

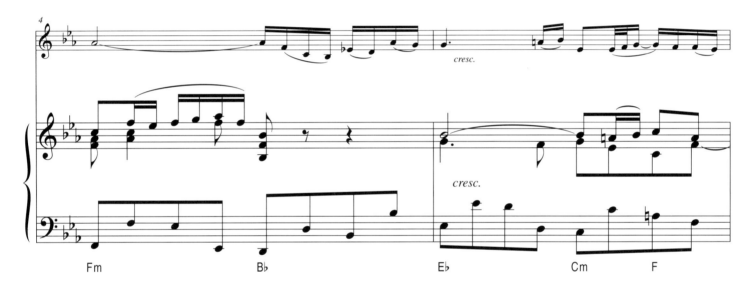

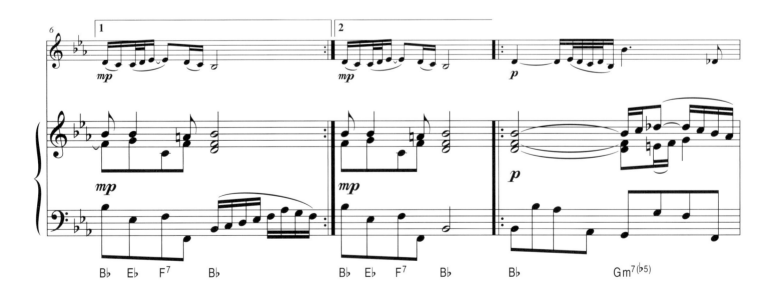

September Song
(from "Knickerbocker Holiday")

Kurt Weill
(1900–1950)
Arr. James Rae

*Tenor Saxophone one octave lower

UE 21 170

Rondeau
(from Abdelazar)

Henry Purcell
(1659–1695)
Arr. James Rae

UE 21 170

All Through the Night

Welsh Traditional
Arr. James Rae

UE 21 170

Autumn Thoughts

Edvard Grieg
(1843–1907)
Arr. James Rae

*Tenor Saxophone one octave lower

UE 21 170

Matt's New Motor

James Rae

UE 21 170

Après un Rêve

Gabriel Fauré
(1845–1924)
Arr. James Rae

*Tenor Saxophone one octave lower

UE 21 170

18

UE 21 170

These Foolish Things

Jack Strachey
and Harry Link
Arr. James Rae

UE 21 170

Habanera
(from Carmen)

Georges Bizet
(1838–1875)
Arr. James Rae

UE 21 170